By Frank Berrios
Illustrated by Shane Clester

 A GOLDEN BOOK • NEW YORK

MARVEL © 2020 MARVEL

All rights reserved. Published by Golden Books, an imprint of Random House Children's Books,
a division of Penguin Random House LLC, 1745 Broadway, New York, NY 10019, and in Canada
by Penguin Random House Canada Limited, Toronto. Golden Books, A Golden Book, A Little Golden Book,
the G colophon, and the distinctive gold spine are registered trademarks of Penguin Random House LLC.
rhcbooks.com
ISBN 978-0-593-17324-4 (trade) — ISBN 978-0-593-17325-1 (ebook)
Printed in the United States of America
10 9 8 7 6 5 4 3 2

I'm **Miles Morales**. I used to have a normal, ordinary life. I lived with my family. I went to school. And I did a lot of homework.

That was until I was
bitten by a weird spider!

I passed out—and when I woke up, I could **STICK TO WALLS!** Crazy!

I could make amazing leaps!

I could turn invisible!

With just a touch of my hand, I could deliver a shocking *venom strike!*

Somehow that spider bite
had given me amazing powers,
just like the original Spider-Man!

I began to realize that the world was starting to need heroes more and more.

There seemed to be new super villains and monsters popping up every day!

At first, I didn't want to be a Super Hero.
I wasn't even sure I could *be* a hero.

But when you have the power to help people, you just have to find it within yourself to do it!

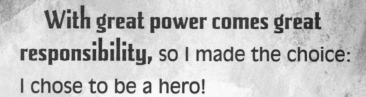

With great power comes great responsibility, so I made the choice: I chose to be a hero!

My best friend, Ganke, is the only person who knows my secret. He even helped me with my first costume.

As the new Spider-Man, I've
taken down a few petty crooks, like
the Kangaroo and the Ringer . . .

It wasn't long before I came to the attention of **Nick Fury**. He is the leader of S.H.I.E.L.D., which is sort of a police force that protects our entire world.

He gave me this new outfit—
with **web-shooters**.

Being the new Spider-Man is awesome!

I'm making new friends. And I think I'm getting the hang of being a hero . . .

. . . but there's nothing easy about saving the world on a school night!